Frankenstein

RETOLD BY PAULINE FRANCIS

READZONE

READZONE BOOKS

First published in this edition 2014

The right of the Author to be identified as the Author of this work has been asserted by the Author in accordance with the Copyright, Designs and Patents Act 1988.

Every attempt has been made by the Publisher to secure appropriate permissions for material reproduced in this book. If there has been any oversight we will be happy to rectify the situation in future editions or reprints. Written submissions should be made to the Publisher.

British Library Cataloguing in Publication Data (CIP) is available for this title.

ISBN 978 1 78322 061 8

Printed in Malta by Melita Press

Cover design and illustration by Emil Dacanay, D.R.Ink
Inside illustrations by Gary Andrews

Visit our website: www.readzonebooks.com

Frankenstein

Introduction

Mary Shelley, born in 1797, is best remembered for her horror story, *Frankenstein*, which was published in 1818.

Mary Shelley married the poet, Percy Shelley, in 1816 and went to live in Italy. In the summer of that year, the Shelleys visited Switzerland with their friend, the poet Lord Byron. It rained so much that the friends decided to entertain each other with ghost stories. Mary went to bed one night, still trying to think of a good story. She woke up, suddenly, terrified after a dream.

"I have found it!" she thought. "What terrified me, will terrify others. I need only describe the ghost that haunted my midnight pillow."

This dream became the story of Frankenstein, which was published two years later.

In 1822, Percy Shelley was drowned when his boat overturned in a storm near the coast of Italy. Mary Shelley returned to England with her son, Percy, and continued writing until her death in 1851.

August, 17––

My dear Sister,

The strangest thing has happened. You will know from my last letter that I am now taking an expedition to the North Pole. Last Monday, our ship was surrounded by ice and fog, and we could not move on.

Of course, we were all very anxious and we had to keep watch on deck. As the fog lifted a little, I saw a sledge in the distance, with a carriage fixed onto it. I stared at it in surprise because the man driving the dogs was at least eight feet tall.

In the morning, when the ice was breaking up, a piece of ice drifted towards our ship. On it was a sledge. O, Margaret, if you could have seen the young man driving this sledge! He was almost frozen to death. When he was able to speak, he told me that he was looking for someone – the tall man I had seen on the strange sledge the day before.

During this past week, he has told me how he came to be so ill and so unhappy. I have written his story down for you, dear Sister, and I send it with this letter.

Your loving Brother,
Robert Walton

CHAPTER ONE

The creature comes alive

My name is Victor Frankenstein, and I have lost everything in the world that is dear to me. I wish I could begin my life again. As you can see, I have suffered great unhappiness. Now that I am about to die, I want to tell you how my life came to be so unhappy.

I had a happy childhood, living by Lake Geneva in Switzerland with my parents, my brothers Ernest and William, and my adopted sister, Elizabeth. The first sadness of my life was the death of my dear mother, the day before I left to go to university in Germany.

It was my chemistry professor there, a kind and gentle man called Mr. Waldman, who told me amazing things that changed my thoughts for ever.

"Modern scientists now know how blood circulates around our bodies," he explained. "They know all about the air we breathe. They have new and great powers."

His words went round and round in my head that night, until my mind was filled with only one thought – I wanted to become a scientist. I went to see Mr. Waldman the very next day and he was pleased to take me on as his student.

"But," he warned me, "if you really want to become a

scientist, you must study every branch of science, including mathematics."

This was a very important moment for me: it decided my whole future.

From that day on, I was only interested in science, especially chemistry. I read the latest books, went to lectures, talked to many people – and Mr. Waldman became a good friend. Sometimes I worked all through the night, and I made fast progress.

I became particularly interested in the human body. I started to collect bones from the graveyards. I cut up dead bodies to find out why they had decayed. I worked day and night in my laboratory, all through a beautiful summer. I almost forgot my friends and family, but they did not complain. My work made me so anxious and so nervous that even a falling leaf made me jump out of my skin. Only my obsession for my work kept me alive.

You will be amazed when I tell you what this work was; but you must believe me. For two years, I had been building a human body – a body that I would bring to life. Yes, I, Victor Frankenstein, would put the spark of electricity into a lifeless body. And it would live!

At last, at one o'clock on a dreary November night, I finished building my human creature. Rain lashed against the windows and my candle had almost gone out. In the flickering light, he lay lifeless at my feet. He was

about eight feet tall, too big I know now; but it was easier
to fit together big body parts.

I could hardly believe what I was doing. This lifeless
creature at my feet would look upon me as its creator.

"Now! Do it now!" I muttered to myself.

Trembling with anxiety, I picked up my instruments and sent a spark of electricity through his body. I waited, hardly able to breathe.

Suddenly, the creature opened its dull yellow eyes, took a deep breath and moved its arms and legs. It was alive! This should have been my greatest moment of happiness. But no! Now he was alive in front of me, I was filled with despair. What had I done?

I forced myself to look at the creature I had worked so hard to make. I was horrified by its shrivelled, yellow skin, by its veins and arteries, by its straight black lips and by its watery, white eyes.

The beauty of the dream vanished. I was disgusted.

I ran to my bedroom and tried to sleep. I had terrible dreams until I awoke, suddenly, shivering with fear. The miserable monster was standing in front of me, lit up by the yellow moon. His eyes, if you could call them eyes, were fixed on me. His jaws opened and a grin wrinkled his cheeks. He tried to speak as he put out his hand to me.

Terrified, I ran out into the street and hid. And all the time, I dreaded to see the dead body that I had brought to life.

CHAPTER TWO

Death on the mountain

I dared not return to my rooms. I walked up and down until morning, drenched by the rain pouring from a black sky. A carriage pulled up outside a nearby inn and, to my surprise, my school friend Henry Clerval got out. He saw me and came straight over to me.

"My dear Frankenstein," he said, "how wonderful to see you. My parents have at last agreed to let me study here."

He stopped speaking and stared at me.

"How pale and ill you look," he said.

He wanted to come to my house and I could not refuse. I hardly knew what I was doing. As I came near, I started to tremble. Would that terrible creature still be alive?

"Wait here!" I said to Henry at the bottom of the stairs.

I ran up to my laboratory and opened the door, trembling. What horror would I see?

The room was empty.

I had breakfast with Henry, but I couldn't sit still. I was filled with horror at what I had done. "That monster will come after me," I thought over and over again, until I was so terrified that I clung to my friend crying, "Save me! Save me!" Then I fell unconscious on the floor.

I was ill for a long time. It was almost two years before I was able to forget my terror and return to my family in Geneva. The day before I started my journey, I received a letter from my father. I read it, threw it on the table and covered my face with my hands.

"My dear Frankenstein," said Henry, "what has happened?"

"My dear little brother, William, has been murdered, strangled on the mountain," I gasped. "He was playing hide−and−seek with Ernest."

I wept.

"Poor William," said Henry sadly, "dear, lovely child! He now sleeps with his angel mother. What are you going to do, Victor?"

"Order the horses," I told him. "I shall go to Geneva at once."

As I came close to my home, I decided to stop at the place where William had died. Lightning streaked around the top of the mountains and a storm broke out. Thunder crashed over my head. Suddenly, in a flash of lightning, I saw a giant figure near the trees. It was hideous and deformed. My teeth chattered and I shivered violently. It was the creature I had brought to life. I watched it climb to the top of the mountains and disappear.

I spent the rest of the night on the mountain, in complete despair. How could I have brought such a creature to life? A creature who had, I was now sure of it, already destroyed someone dear to me? In the morning, I went home and wept with my unhappy family.

"At least the murderer has been arrested," Ernest told me.

"No, it is not possible," I replied. "I saw him on the mountain last night."

"Him?" my brother asked. "Justine killed William. She had our mother's portrait in her pocket. William was wearing it when he died."

He began to weep.

"How could she?" he cried. "She has nursed him from babyhood!"

"You are all wrong," I said. "I know the murderer. Justine is innocent."

But after a short trial the next day, Justine was sentenced to death and executed. I watched my family weep at her grave. She and William were the first victims of my success.

CHAPTER THREE

Horror on the glacier

Nothing could take my sadness away. I couldn't sleep. William was dead, Justine was dead, and I wished that I could die too. I was filled with guilt. I was in hell.

My father was worried about me.

"Do not grieve too long," he said, "William would not want you to be so unhappy."

But his words had no effect. I wanted to be alone all the time. I took a boat out on Lake Geneva hour after hour and stared down at the water. I would have drowned myself, but the thought of my family's unhappiness stopped me.

About two months after William's murder, I decided to travel in the nearby mountains. I hoped that the beauty of the scenery would make me forget all the horror of the past months. I climbed as high as the Valley of Chamonix. There, a long–lost feeling of joy came over me from time to time as I watched the sun sparkle on the glacier all around me.

Then I decided to walk slowly across the ice. Mountains rose in front of me. Their icy and glittering peaks shone in the sunlight over the clouds. It was beautiful.

Suddenly, to my great surprise, a tall figure came towards me with superhuman speed. I almost fainted with terror. I stared at him. I could not believe my eyes.

It was *my* creature!

I trembled with anger and horror. He came nearer, and I looked away. His face was almost too horrible for human eyes.

I wanted to kill him.

"You devil!" I shouted at him. "How dare you come near me? If only *your* death would bring my brother back to life!"

To my astonishment, the creature spoke to me. How did he know the words?

"You created me, yet now you hate me," he said. "How dare *you* play with life in this way? If you do as I ask, I will leave you and your family in peace."

I jumped on him.

"Let me kill you now!" I begged.

He ran back from me and spoke again.

"Don't you think I have suffered enough?" he cried. "I see happy people everywhere, but I can't be part of their lives. I *was* good, but unhappiness has changed me into an evil creature. I could fight you easily; but you are my master, my king. Make me happy again, then I will be good again."

"Go away," I replied. "We are enemies."

"How can I make you feel kindness towards me?" the creature asked. "Everybody hates me, even you. I have walked in these mountains and glaciers for days. I am so alone and unhappy. But you can help me. Listen to me, please. Then you can decide what to do with me."

I followed him across the ice as he spoke. I wanted to know only one thing – had *he* killed William? I would have to listen. We came to a small hut on the mountain side, and there I sat and listened to the creature's story.

CHAPTER FOUR

The creature's story

"I was very frightened when I first came alive," said the creature. The light dazzled me and I had to close my eyes. But then I was afraid of the darkness. I ran from your laboratory towards the forest. I was too hot and I went into the forest to find shade. I lay down by a stream and wept. Later that day, when it was dark, I was too cold.

Within a few days, my eyes had become used to the dark and the light. I started to walk further into the forest. I moved all the time, looking for food. One day, I came to a village. But men came and threw stones at me, and beat me with pieces of wood. I ran back through the forest until I found an empty cottage. I decided to stay there to hide from the cold – and from the cruelty of the people around me.

I soon discovered that a blind old man and his son and daughter lived in the cottage next to mine. I wanted to speak to them, but I knew that they would be afraid of me. Instead, I watched them and learned as much as I could from them. They were always cold and hungry like me, and I did all I could to help them. I was a good person then. During the night, I collected firewood and left them in front of their door. In this way, they had more time to grow vegetables.

One day, I understood why people hated me so much. I saw my face for the first time in a pool of clear water. I was terrified! I could not believe my own eyes. I was used to the beauty of my neighbours. I was hideous. I could not show my face to them yet.

I listened to the sounds they made and learned the words I speak to you now. Sometimes, Felix read to his father, and his sister Agatha, by the light of a candle. I did not understand this for a long time, until I realised that he was reading many of the words that he spoke.

And what was my life like? I slept during the day when my neighbours worked. When they slept, I went into the wood to collect wood and food. As summer came, I began to forget how unhappy my life had been.

My neighbours were kind and gentle people. I practised their language every day.

"They will become my dear friends," I told myself, "Soon I will be able to talk to them. They will forget how ugly I am. I will be happy at last."

One day, a beautiful lady dressed in black rode up to the cottage and asked to see Felix. She did not speak their language very well. When Felix came out to meet her, his eyes shone with happiness. Her name was Safie. She stayed and, like the sun, chased away the clouds. Every evening, Felix taught Safie history and geography, and they read together.

"If I listen, I can learn too," I thought.

Every conversation between Felix and Safie taught me new ideas and new feelings. When they talked of war and murder, I felt great disgust. And when they talked of family and beauty, I realised that there was nobody else in the world like me. I was a monster.

One day, when the old man was alone, I made up my mind. This was my chance to talk to him. I knocked on his door.

"Who is there?" asked the old man. "Come in."

I went in. He was kind and let me rest by the fire, and we began to talk.

"I am an unhappy creature," I said, "I have no relations or friends."

"I am blind and I cannot judge you by your face," replied the old man, "but your words make me believe that you are sincere. I am a poor man but I will help you in any way that I can."

He was the only man who had ever spoken kindly to me. I started to speak. Then I heard footsteps outside the door. I hadn't a moment to lose. I seized the old man's

hand and cried, "Save and protect me! Please be my friend!"

The cottage door opened. Felix, Agatha and Safie came in, their faces full of horror as they looked at me. Agatha fainted. Safie ran outside. I clung to the old man's knees, "Help me! Help me!" I begged. Felix ran over to us. With sudden strength, he pulled me away from his father and threw me onto the ground. He picked up a stick and hit me, over and over again.

I could have ripped him to pieces on the spot, like a lion rips an antelope. But I was too upset by the loss of my dear friends. Instead I left their cottage and crept back to my own. I wanted to die. And I began to curse the man who had created me.

What could I do? I didn't want to be hunted like an animal. I had no choice but to move on again. Then a thought crossed my mind. You were my creator, you lived in Geneva. I decided to come to ask you for help. After all, you gave me my life and my feelings.

On the hills outside your city, I met a beautiful child.

"This child is young," I told myself, "he does not know yet how cruel people can be. I could keep him as my friend. Then I won't be alone."

I caught hold of the boy's arm. He screamed and struggled and shouted, "My papa is Mr. Frankenstein. He will punish you."

"Frankenstein!" I repeated. "The man who left me alone in a world that hates me! You shall be my first victim."

I strangled him.

As I left the mountain, I saw a barn. I went inside and found a young girl asleep. I put the portrait of your mother in her pocket. Oh yes, I had already learned from my fellow men how to cause trouble. I knew she would be blamed for the murder.

The creature looked straight at me, and I saw every wrinkle, every mark of his hideous face – the face I had created.

"I am a lonely and unhappy man, " he cried, "no woman will ever love me. You must create a friend for me – a female. You cannot refuse."

The creature suddenly stopped speaking and waited for my answer.

CHAPTER FIVE
The second creature

I was almost mad with rage when the creature came to the end of his story.

"I *do* refuse," I told him at last, "even if you torture me, I will not do it."

"You are wrong," this fiend replied. " If I cannot fill people with love, then I will fill them with fear. Especially you, because you created me."

As he spoke, he became so angry that his face was even more ugly. Then he was ashamed of his anger.

"I am asking only a very small thing – a female creature. I know we will be monsters cut off from the world. Our lives may not be happy, but they will be harmless. We will go to South America."

He looked more closely at me.

"I can see from your eyes that you feel sorry for me."

"But what if you come back here?" I asked. "The evil in you will come back."

We argued together like this for a long time. Until at last, I agreed to his request. And as soon as I told him this, the creature disappeared from my sight across the glacier. I walked down the mountain in the starry twilight. It was beautiful. I begin to cry. I was in hell again.

I put off the evil job for as long as possible. I went out on the lake every day and lay watching the clouds or the waves rippling around my boat. I was almost happy again.

One day, my father came to speak to me.

"I am happy, dear son," he began, "to see that you are more like your usual self. Now is the time to tell you something." He hesitated. "From the day we adopted Elizabeth, I have always hoped that you would marry her."

"Yes, I love her very much," I told him.

"Then let the wedding take place straight away," my father suggested.

My happy mood disappeared at once. I remembered my promise to the creature, and the danger that I would bring to my family if I did not keep it. I could not marry Elizabeth now, not with the weight of this secret hanging around my neck. I must let the monster leave with his mate before I could look forward to my own happiness.

I decided to go to England at once to finish my work.

"I will marry Elizabeth as soon as I come back," I told my father.

"Do not stay away too long," he answered, "I am not getting any younger."

I was afraid of one thing. Would my family be safe while I was away — safe from my creature? Even my friend Henry Clerval would not be there to protect them! He wanted to travel with me.

On the journey to England, I realised how unhappy I really was. Henry was delighted by everything he saw. He was glad to be alive. He was a constant reminder of how I used to be. I hardly went out with him. I needed the time to collect everything for my new creation. This was a torture to me, like a single drop of water falling on my head.

I decided to finish my work on the Orkney Islands, near the Scottish coast. I rented a lonely, miserable hut with two rooms, a wretched place that suited my unhappiness very well.

Every day, my work became harder and harder. Sometimes I could hardly bare to step inside my laboratory. I was enthusiastic, it is true, when I had made my first creation; but now I knew the horror of what I was doing. I became nervous and restless. I was afraid every moment – afraid that my first creature would appear to torment me again.

One evening, when it was too dark to work any more, I sat and thought about what I was doing. What if this new creature was ten thousand times more evil than her mate? What if she took pleasure in murder? He had promised to hide away from the rest of the world; but she had not made that promise. What if they hated each other? Then another terrible thought entered my head.

"They might have children!" I cried. "Then I will have brought these monsters into the world for ever!"

As I had these thoughts, the moon came out. I looked up at the window as the moonlight flooded in. I cried out in surprise. There at the window I saw the ghastly face of my monster, his lips wrinkled into a terrible grin.

He had followed me!

At that moment, I knew that I could not create another creature like him. As he watched, I tore to pieces his future mate.

CHAPTER SIX

Death of a friend

The creature howled with despair as I destroyed my work. He did not even try to stop me. Then he disappeared.

I sat gazing out to sea for many hours. Apart from a gentle breeze on the water, there was no sound. Suddenly, I heard a boat came to the shore near my hut. A few minutes later, my door creaked, as if someone was trying to open it quietly.

I began to tremble from head to foot. I wanted to run away or call on my neighbour for help. But I couldn't move. I waited. Soon the door of my room slowly opened.

The monster stood in front of me.

"You have broken your promise," he said quietly, "I have been through terrible hunger and cold to follow you here. You have destroyed my hopes."

"Go away!" I shouted at him. "Yes, I have broken my promise. I will never make another creature like you, so ugly and so wicked."

The monster's voice became angry.

"Remember that I have the power!" he said. "I can make you so unhappy that you will not want to live. You are my creator, but I am your master. You must obey me."

"Go away!" I shouted. "You will only make me angrier if you stay."

He said something that I can never forget.

"I go. But, remember, I shall be with you on your wedding night."

He left me. Why had I let him go? Why hadn't I killed him? I shivered as his words echoed in my head. *"Remember, I shall be with you on your wedding night."*

"So that is how this will end," I told myself. "With my death. And what will my poor Elizabeth do then?"

I wept until the sun rose over the sea, then slept. I felt calmer when I woke up, and my anger turned to unhappiness. The morning boat brought a letter came from Clerval, begging me to return with him to Geneva. I decided to leave the island.

I shuddered. There was a job I had to do before I left my hut. I forced myself to go back into the horror of my laboratory. The remains of the half-finished creature lay on the floor. It looked like the mangled flesh of a living person. I gathered up the pieces, placed them in a basket with some heavy stones and set out for the mainland in my boat.

I was so tired that I fell asleep in my boat and drifted out to sea. I woke up hot and thirsty.

"So the sea is to be my grave!" I thought sadly.

The sea became rough and I was sick. Then to my joy, I saw land ahead. But when I came to the shore, my joy did not last very long. There were men standing on the seashore and they pulled me roughly from my boat.

"Why are you so rude?" I asked. "Is it your custom to treat strangers in this way?"

"You must come to Mr. Kirwin, to explain yourself," said one of the men.

"Who is Mr. Kirwin?" I asked, surprised. "And where am I?"

"You are in Ireland," said the man, "and Mr. Kirwin is the magistrate. Perhaps you can explain the death of a gentleman found murdered here last night."

I followed the man, unaware of the horror that was waiting for me. I heard more about the murder. A young man of about twenty–five had been strangled. I started to tremble as I remembered my poor brother, William.

"Now we shall show you the body," said the magistrate.

I was taken to an inn. I entered the room where the corpse lay and was led up to the coffin. When I remember that terrible moment, I still shudder in horror.

In front of me lay the lifeless body of my dear friend, Henry Clerval.

CHAPTER SEVEN

The promise

I remained half-conscious for two months in prison, crying out in my fever, "I have murdered William, Justine, Clerval!" Sometimes I felt the creature's fingers round my own neck and rose from my bed to fight him off. Oh why didn't I die like the others?

I was strong. One day, I woke up and remembered what had happened. I groaned quietly to myself. If only it had all been a dream!

"I have sent for your father," the magistrate told me kindly.

"Then why hasn't he arrived?" I cried out in terror. "Has someone killed him, too?"

But my father arrived soon afterwards.

"Are you all safe?" I asked him. "You, and Elizabeth – and Ernest?"

"Yes," my father replied, "we are all well."

His visit helped me to cover more quickly from my fever; but it was followed by the darkest depression. I wanted to die. I sat for hours without moving or speaking. One day, the magistrate came to see me.

"You are free to leave," he told me. "It has been proved that you were on the Orkney Islands at the time of your friend's death."

"You can return to Geneva when you are well," my father said. "Elizabeth and Ernest are waiting for you."

"I want to go now," I told him.

I could not tell my father why. I felt it was my duty to look after them, to protect them from this murderer. And if I could find him, I would kill him.

"No," said my father, "you are too ill. You look like a skeleton, and you are burning with fever."

I insisted and we sailed soon afterwards to France. I lay on the deck looking up at the stars.

"My past is just a bad dream," I told myself.

But I could not forget that terrible night when the creature had first lived. I began to weep bitterly. That night, I dreamed of the monster's hands around my neck and cried out in my sleep.

"We will rest in Paris," said my father, worried by my state of mind.

In that beautiful city, he tried to cheer me up with visits and friends; but I could not bear to go out.

"You do not know me very well, father," I said one day. "I murdered William, Justine and Henry."

"Dear Victor," he replied, "do not say such things."

"It is true!" I cried.

My father changed the subject. He thought that I still had a fever, or that I was mad. He never let me speak in this way again.

I received a letter from Elizabeth soon after this conversation.

MY DEAR FRIEND,

I hope to see you in less than a fortnight.

But before we meet, there is something I must explain to you. As you know, our parents always hoped that we would marry. Are you completely sure that you love me more than just as a sister? Are you sure that you are not in love with somebody else?

Why do I ask you this? It is because last year you were so unhappy and longed to travel, to get away from everyone you knew.

I love you. But I can only marry you if you wish it too.

Do not answer me now. When we meet, I shall know if you love me.

ELIZABETH LAVENZA
Geneva, May 18th, 17—

Unfortunately, this letter reminded me immediately of the creature's last words to me: "*I will be with you on your wedding night.*"

"He will do everything to destroy our happiness, by killing me!" I wept. "But then I will be at peace at last. And if I, in the struggle, kill him, then I will be free from him."

I wrote back to Elizabeth.

MY DEAR ELIZABETH

I love you – but I have one secret, Elizabeth – a dreadful one. You will be horrified when you know it. You will be amazed that I could have lived with it for so long. I will tell you this secret the day after our wedding.

I ask you not to mention it before then.
VICTOR

I felt happier when I had written this letter.

"No, I shall *not* put off the marriage," I told myself. "Let the monster do as he wishes. I am ready to meet him."

36

CHAPTER EIGHT

Murder by the lake

Elizabeth did everything she could to help me when I returned to Geneva. Sometimes, I had bad dreams, feverish illnesses and great rages. Memory brought madness with it. At other times, I did not speak at all. She was always gentle and kind. She wept with me and for me. But there is no peace for the guilty.

Soon after my arrival, my father began to talk about our marriage. I stayed silent.

"Have you met somebody else you wish to marry?" he asked at last.

"No, of course not," I replied. "I love Elizabeth and I look forward to our wedding day. Let us choose the day now. In life or in death, I wish only for her happiness."

"My dear Victor, do not say such things," said my father. "We have had much unhappiness; but you will have children who will replace the people we have lost so cruelly."

"We shall marry in ten days," I said as cheerfully as I could.

If only I had known the horror that my enemy had planned, I would have left my country immediately and wandered the world where no one knew me. I did not fear my own death. How *could* I have known that I was putting someone close to me in such danger?

As my wedding day came nearer, I felt my heart sink. I hid my worries from my father and Elizabeth. I secretly carried pistols and a dagger wherever I went in case the fiend attacked me. I was always on guard.

The wedding ceremony took place with great happiness, although I saw a strange look of fear pass over Elizabeth's face. Was she thinking about the dreadful secret that I had promised to tell her the next day? Or did she somehow know the other horror that was to come?

After the ceremony, Elizabeth and I travelled to the town of Evian, on Lake Geneva, where we had planned to spend our first night. They were the last moments of happiness I ever had. We enjoyed the beauty of the lake as we sailed. In the distance, the sun sparkled on the snow at the top of Mont Blanc. I took Elizabeth's hand.

"I have suffered more than you can imagine," I told her, "but now I can enjoy the happiness of this one day."

"Be happy, my dear Victor," Elizabeth replied, "and look at all this beauty. It is a wonderful day. I am very happy, even if my face is sometimes sad."

When we reached the town, and darkness began to fall, my fears returned – fears that would soon would be with me for ever. It was eight o' clock when the boat landed and we walked for a short time by the shores of the lake. Then we went to the inn and watched the moon rise over the mountains.

Suddenly, the wind began to howl and clouds raced across the moon. Waves ran across the surface of the lake, and heavy rain began to fall. Now a thousand fears rose in my mind. As every sound terrified me, I touched the pistol hidden inside my coat.

"My dear Victor," said Elizabeth, "what are you afraid of?"

"This night, my love," I replied.

I dreaded the fight that was to come. I did not want my wife to see it.

"Go to bed," I told her.

She left me, and I walked through every passage in that inn, looking into every corner that could hide my enemy. I did not find anyone and I began to feel calmer. Perhaps my creature had forgotten his threat! Perhaps he did not want to hurt me, his creator, after all. How could I have been so stupid!

A terrible scream filled the air as I made my way back to our rooms. It came from our bedroom. As I heard it, I could hear my blood pounding in my veins as the truth rushed to my mind. I froze on the spot until there was another scream. Then I rushed into our room.

Oh why didn't I die then? Why am I still here, telling you this story? She, the purest creature on earth, was lying lifeless across the bed, her pale and twisted face half-covered by her hair. Everywhere I go, I still see her. How could I look at her and live? I fell to the ground, unconscious.

CHAPTER NINE
My search begins

When I opened my eyes, I was surrounded by the people from the inn. I ran from them to our bedroom – to Elizabeth's body. Someone had covered her face and neck with a handkerchief. I went over to her and took her in my arms. For a moment, I thought she was just asleep. Then I saw the finger prints of the murderer on her skin.

As I wept by her side, I looked up. It was dark outside, apart from a yellow moon, and at the window I saw the grinning face of my monster. He pointed towards the corpse of my wife. I took out my pistol and fired at him; but he ran away and I watched him dive into the lake below.

I went after him, with men from the inn; but he had completely disappeared. I crawled back to my bedroom and wept by my dead wife's side. I was in a state of terror… the death of William, the execution of Justine… the murder of Clerval, and now the murder of my wife.

"I can see Ernest, dead at the monster's feet. The creature is holding my father. He is going to murder him!" I screamed.

These thoughts forced me into action. I hired a boat

and men to row me back to Geneva. I passed the same mountains I had watched yesterday with Elizabeth. The rain had stopped and it was beautiful.

"A monster has snatched away from me any hope of happiness," I wept again. "I have never been so unhappy."

On my return, I went straight to the magistrate and told him my story.

"Please help me to hunt down the murderer," I begged him.

"I cannot," he replied, "we do not have the men who could hunt down such a creature, a creature who can walk over ice and live in caves unknown to man. I am sorry."

My father could not take in any more horror, and he died a few days later in my arms. I sat at the tomb where my dear family was buried. Anger soon took place of my grief. I knelt on the grass and kissed the earth.

"I swear on this holy earth to hunt down this devil and fight until one of us dies," I cried. "Let him feel the agony that I now feel."

As I finished speaking, a terrible laugh rang through the air. It echoed and re−echoed around the mountains and hurt my ears. I felt that I was in hell. The laughter died away and that terrible voice whispered in my ear:

"I am satisfied," he whispered. "You have decided to live, and I am satisfied."

Suddenly, the full moon shone on his ugly, twisted body as he ran away. I went after him.

I have been searching for him ever since. Sometimes, the monster left this message for me on the barks of trees, or cut in stone.

"MY REIGN IS NOT YET OVER.
YOU LIVE − MY POWER IS COMPLETE.
FOLLOW ME, MY ENEMY,
WE STILL HAVE TO FIGHT."

I shall never give up my search until the day I die.

And now I have reached the end of my story, dear friend, and I am very tired.

September 12th

My beloved Sister,

It is midnight and I write to tell you that Victor died today. Before he died, he made me promise to hunt down and kill his creature. I have wept over his body. He has become a true friend in the week that I have known him.

Margaret, as I write these words, I can hear a strange voice coming from Frankenstein's cabin. I must go and look! Good night, my sister...

Good God! What a scene has just taken place! I can hardly believe that is has happened. I can now tell you the end of Frankenstein's story, although I hardly have the strength to write it.

I went into the cabin where Frankenstein's body lay. Over him hung a shape which I cannot find the words to describe – a gigantic and hideous man, his face hidden under long ragged hair. He was reaching out with his hand, a hand no different from that of a mummy.

He was howling with grief. He was horrible, loathsome, repulsive. But I remembered my promise to Frankenstein.

"Stay!" I called out.

He paused and looked at me in amazement, then at the body again.

"Oh, Frankenstein, forgive me!" he wailed over the body. "I have destroyed you by destroying all those you love."

He spoke to me of his misery, his desire for love and friendship.

"You hate me, I can see that," he said, staring straight at me, "but not as much as I hate myself. Do not worry. You will see no more of me. I shall go as far north as possible on my ice raft. And there I shall die."

The creature looked down at Frankenstein once more.

"Farewell, Frankenstein! My unhappiness will end with my death. Farewell."

He jumped from the cabin window as he said this, and the waves carried him away. He was soon lost in the darkness.

I hope that this is the end of my tale of horror, dear Sister. There is nothing more to say until I see you soon in England.

Your loving Brother,
Robert Walton

Glossary

Key:

adj	adjective
adv	adverb
n	noun
phr	phrase
phr v	phrasal verb
(superl)	superlative
vi	intransitive verb
vt	transitive verb

adopted	*adj*	an adopted child is someone else's child that you have taken, legally, into your own family	7
agony	*n*	great pain or suffering	42
antelope	*n*	an African animal like a deer	23
artery	*n*	one of the two main types of tube that carry blood in the body	10
be blamed, to	*passive*	if someone is blamed for something, people say that they are responsible for it	24
be executed, to	*passive*	to be killed as a punishment	14
be sentenced death, to	*passive* *phr*	if someone is sentenced to death, a court finds them guilty of a crime and decides they must die	14

chatter, to	*vi*	to make a noise by clicking your teeth together, usually when you are cold or frightened	12
corpse	*n*	a dead body	32
creak, to	*vi*	to make a short, fairly high-pitched noise	29
curse, to	*vt*	if you curse someone, you mean that you hope that bad things will happen to them	23
decay, to	*vi*	to rot	8
deformed	*adj*	if something is deformed, it doesn't have its usual shape	12
dreadful	*adj*	awful; horrible	36
dreary	*adj*	miserable; dull and unpleasant	8
drenched	*adj*	soaked; very, very wet	11
duty	*n*	something you have to do	34
echo, to	*vi*	if something echoes, it repeats itself	30
feverish	*adj*	having a high body temperature	37
fiend	*n*	a very cruel person; a devil	25
flickering	*adj*	unsteady; blowing	8
froze	*past simple of freeze;vi*	stopped moving immediately	40

glacier	*n*	a large area of ice in the mountains	15
graveyard	*n*	the area around a church where dead people are buried	8
grieve, to	*vi*	to be very sad, especially when someone has died	15
hideous	*adj*	very ugly	20
inn	*n* *(old-fashioned)*	a pub with rooms where you can sleep	11
jump out of one's skin, to	*phr*	to make a sudden movement because something frightens you.	8
keep watch, to	*phr*	to watch and listen all the time in case something bad happens	5
lash, to	*vt*	to hit hard	8
latest	*adj* *(superl)*	most recent	8
loathsome	*adj*	hateful	45
long- lost	*adj*	something long-lost is something that you haven't had or seen for a long time	15
magistrate	*n*	a judge	32
mangled	*adj*	if something is mangled, it is badly damaged, so that you can't see what it originally looked like	30
mate	*n*	a partner	27

mummy	*n*	a preserved, dried body	44
on deck	*phr*	outside on a ship	5
on guard	*phr*	watching out for anything dangerous that might happen	38
on the spot	*phr*	immediately	23
peak	*n*	a mountain top	15
pound, to	*vi*	to beat very hard	40
raft	*n*	a kind of simple, small, flat boat	45
ripple, to	*vi*	when water ripples, it has small, gentle waves on the surface	26
shrivelled	*adj*	if something is shrivelled, it is dry, smaller than it was and wrinkled	10
sink: I felt my heart sink	*phr*	if your heart sinks, you become depressed	38
skeleton	*n*	all the bones of a person or animal	34
sledge	*n*	a kind of small cart used for carrying things over snow or ice	5
snatch away, to	*phr*	to take something away suddenly and violently	42
strangle, to	*vt*	to kill someone by squeezing their throat	24
struggle, to	*vi*	to move violently	23
take someone on, to	*phr v*	to employ someone	7

threat	*n*	something that you say you will do to harm someone, unless they do as you tell them	40
torture, to	*vt*	to hurt someone repeatedly, for example to make them give you some information you want	25
twilight	*n*	half light, after the sun has gone down	25
twisted	*adj*	made ugly with pain	40
wretched	*adj*	miserable; dreary	27

Frankenstein Test Yourself

Exercise 1

Match the descriptions to the names below.

1   Margaret's brother
2   the blind man's son
3   the monster's creator
4   Victor's adopted sister
5   Felix's sister
6   Victor's brother
7   Victor's friend
8   She was accused of William's murder.
9   Felix's friend
10   Victor's professor

a   Frankenstein
b   Safie
c   Mr Waldman
d   Robert Walton
e   Agatha
f   Henry Clerval
g   Elizabeth
h   Felix
i   Justine
j   William

Exercise 2

Are these sentences true (T) or false (F)?

1   Frankenstein received a letter from Clerval in which Clerval asked him to stay on the island.

2   When Frankenstein's boat came to shore, he was in Ireland.

3   The monster killed Clerval.

4   Elizabeth wrote to tell Frankenstein that she no longer loved him.

5   Elizabeth and Victor got married in the town of Evian.

6   When Frankenstein returned to his bedroom, he discovered that the monster had killed his wife.

7   The magistrate promised to help Frankenstein hunt down the monster.

8   Frankenstein's father died several months after Elizabeth's murder.

9   The monster often left messages for Frankenstein.

10   Robert killed the monster.

Answers

Exercise 1   1 d; 2 h; 3 a; 4 g; 5 e; 6 j; 7 f; 8 i; 9 b; 10 c

Exercise 2   1 T; 2 T; 3 T; 4 F; 5 F; 6 T; 7 F; 8 F; 9 T; 10 F